The Three Latkes

For my friends at Maimonides School
—E.A.K.

For J.P.D., J.E.M., and L.B.
—F.P.T.

KAR-BEN PUBLISHING®
An imprint of Lerner Publishing Group, Inc.
241 First Avenue North
Minneapolis, MN 55401 USA

Website address: www.karben.com

Main body text set in Kidprint MT Std.
Typeface provided by Monotype Typography.

Library of Congress Cataloging-in-Publication Data

Names: Kimmel, Eric A., author. | Parker Thomas, Feronia, illustrator.
Title: The three latkes / by Eric A. Kimmel ; illustrations by Feronia Parker-Thomas.
Description: Minneapolis : Kar-Ben Publishing, [2021]. | Audience: Ages 4–8 | Audience: Grades K–1 | Summary: "When three Hanukkah latkes fight over which of them tastes the best, the winner is decided by the family cat. Which does he choose?"— Provided by publisher.
Identifiers: LCCN 2020041828 (print) | LCCN 2020041829 (ebook) | ISBN 9781541588912 | ISBN 9781541588929 (paperback) | ISBN 9781728428987 (ebook)
Subjects: LCSH: Latkes—Juvenile humor. | Jewish cooking—Juvenile humor. | Hanukkah cooking—Juvenile humor.
Classification: LCC PN6231.L327 K56 2021 (print) | LCC PN6231.L327 (ebook) | DDC 818/.602—dc23

LC record available at https://lccn.loc.gov/2020041828
LC ebook record available at https://lccn.loc.gov/2020041829

Manufactured in the United States of America
1-47455-48020-12/29/2020

The Three Latkes

Eric A. Kimmel

Illustrations by Feronia Parker-Thomas

KAR-BEN
PUBLISHING

ONCE UPON A TIME, THERE WERE THREE LATKES.

A red latke, a yellow latke, and a gold latke.
On the first night of Hanukkah, they began
talking excitedly.

Red Latke said, "I am made with red potatoes. I'm the best."

"I am made with yellow potatoes," said Yellow Latke. "I'm the best."

Gold Latke said, "I am made with gold potatoes. That makes me the best."

"I am fried in vegetable oil. That's where I get my beautiful color," boasted Red Latke.

The three latkes argued and argued.
They couldn't decide which one of them was the best.

Finally, Yellow Latke said, "Let's ask the cat. The cat knows all about food. Whenever there's food left on the floor, the cat licks it up."

"Good idea!" said Red Latke and Gold Latke. "We'll ask the cat!"

The three latkes hopped off the table.

"Please help us out, Kitty. Which of us latkes is the best? Is it Red Latke, Yellow Latke, or Gold Latke?"

"I don't know," said the clever cat.
"I'll have to taste each of you. But I
like my latkes with a yummy topping."

"You can dip me in applesauce," offered Red Latke.

The cat dipped Red Latke into the sweet applesauce and ate him up. "Yum!" said the cat, licking her lips.

"Wait! You haven't tasted me yet," said Yellow Latke.
"I'll taste great with sour cream."

The cat dipped Yellow Latke into the smooth sour cream . . .

"Double yum!"
purred the cat.

"Don't forget about me!" shouted Gold Latke. "Try me with jam!"
The cat smeared Gold Latke with strawberry jam and ate him up.

"Triple yum!" said the cat. "Now that I've tasted all the latkes, I'm ready to decide which latke is the best. The best latke is . . ."

But nobody knows what the cat said.
There were no latkes left to hear the answer.

People still argue about which latkes are best, what kind of oil to use for frying, and whether to eat them with applesauce, sour cream, or jam.

But the one who really knows is the clever cat. And all she says is . . .

"MEOW!"

Very Best Latkes

INGREDIENTS

½ onion
1½ pounds potatoes (red, yellow, or gold)
2 eggs
¼ cup flour
3 teaspoons salt
oil (vegetable, schmaltz, or peanut) for frying

DIRECTIONS

1. Grate the onion.

2. Grate the potatoes. Immediately place the grated potatoes in a bowl of cold water.

3. Place the eggs, flour, onion, and salt in a separate bowl. Drain the grated potatoes well, and add the rest of the ingredients. Mix well.

4. Heat the oil in a frying pan over medium heat. Test the oil by dropping a tiny bit of the potato mixture into the pan. When the oil sizzles, it is ready.

5. Drop the mixture by spoonfuls into the oil. Press down gently with the back of a spatula to flatten. Fry 2 to 3 minutes until golden. Then flip the latkes, and fry 1 to 2 minutes on the second side. Repeat until all the potato mixture has been used. (You will need to add more oil to the pan every couple of batches.)

This recipe makes about 16 latkes. Be sure to have an adult help you with the frying.